Feathertop

BASED ON THE TALE BY NATHANIEL HAWTHORNE

By Robert D. San Souci • Illustrated by Daniel San Souci

A Doubleday Book for Young Readers

For Rose O'Neil
with boundless love
from both of us
—RSS
—DSS

A Doubleday Book for Young Readers
Published by Delacorte Press
Bantam Doubleday Dell Publishing Group, Inc.,
666 Fifth Avenue, New York, New York 10103
DOUBLEDAY
and the portrayal of an anchor with a dolphin
are trademarks of Bantam Doubleday Dell
Publishing Group, Inc.

Library of Congress
Cataloging in Publication Data
San Souci, Robert.
Feathertop : based on the tale by Nathaniel Hawthorne / by
Robert D. San Souci; illustrated by Daniel San Souci.—1st ed.
    p.   cm.
Based on: Mother Rigby / by Nathaniel Hawthorne.
Summary: When a witch creates a scarecrow and uses him
to play a joke on the local judge, the judge's daughter falls in
love with the scarecrow.
ISBN 0-385-42044-7.
[1. Scarecrows—Fiction.   2. Witches—Fiction.]
I. San Souci, Daniel, ill.   II. Hawthorne, Nathaniel,
1804-1864. Mother Rigby.   III. Title.
PZ7.S1947Fe   1992
[Fic]—dc20   91-10104   CIP   AC

RL: 4.1
Manufactured in U.S.A.
October 1992
10 9 8 7 6 5 4 3 2 1
FSL

Robert and Daniel San Souci

have together published many award-winning books with Doubleday, including *The Legend of Scarface*—A *New York Times* Best Illustrated Book, *The Legend of Sleepy Hollow,* and most recently, *The Christmas Ark.*

While continuing to collaborate, the brothers also produce works independently. Robert's *Larger Than Life* has received wide acclaim, as has Daniel's *North Country Night,* which was selected as a "Pick of the Lists" by *American Bookseller.*

Both Robert and Daniel San Souci live in the San Francisco Bay area.

AUTHOR'S NOTE:

This tale by Nathaniel Hawthorne was first published in *The International Magazine* in 1852 under the title "Feathertop: A Moralized Legend." In adapting the tale, I have sought to retain as much of the original style and spirit of the story as possible. The somewhat changed ending was inspired by a quotation (used here as the epigraph) from Hawthorne's own notebooks.

The illustrations offer details of costume and setting that reflect the life and look of colonial New England in the 1750s.

The paintings in this book were done using Windsor Newton watercolors on 140 lb. cold-press watercolor paper.

The text of this book is set in 18 point ITC Garamond Book Condensed, a contemporary cutting of the 16th-century classic design of Claude Garamond.

Typography by Lynn Braswell.

"…we are not endowed with real life, and all that seems most real about us is but the thinnest substance of a dream—till the heart be touched. That touch creates us."

—Nathaniel Hawthorne,
FROM HIS NOTEBOOKS

ON A MORNING near the end of October, Mother Rigby, one of the most powerful witches in early New England, rose with the sun. She planned to build a scarecrow to put in the middle of her corn patch. The crows and blackbirds had discovered the ripe ears of Indian corn and feasted morning and evening on the plump multicolored kernels.

While Dickon, her cat, watched, Mother Rigby crooked her little finger. Immediately, an old broomstick flew across the room and hovered in the air in front of her.

"This will make an excellent backbone for my scarecrow," she said. Then she yelled *"Scat!"* at the naughty cat, who was using the broom handle as a scratching post. Dickon gave an annoyed *"Meow!"* and leapt on top of the battered old leather-bound trunk in the corner to begin his morning wash.

Mother Rigby wiggled more fingers. A forked tree limb floated in the window to become the scarecrow's right arm. A rolling pin and wooden spoon arrived from the kitchen cupboard to become the other arm, joining themselves to form an elbow. For the right leg, a hoe handle, and for the left, a thin stick from the woodpile, together danced in through the open back door of the cottage.

For the body, Mother Rigby conjured a worn meal bag stuffed with straw. For the head, she summoned a large pumpkin. She cut holes for the eyes, a slit for the mouth, popped a blue button in the middle for a nose, then set the pumpkin on top of the broomstick neck.

"I've seen worse heads on many a pair of shoulders in town," laughed the witch. "But it's clothes that make the man!"

She clapped her hands, and the battered old trunk, carrying a protesting Dickon, slid to her side. While the cat climbed onto her shoulder, Mother Rigby lifted out an ancient plum-colored coat. Once it had been very elegant, but now it was faded and tattered. She put this on her scarecrow.

Next she presented him a pair of threadbare scarlet breeches, a pair of worn silk stockings that snagged and sagged upon his wooden legs, and shoes with tarnished silver buckles.

Last, she blew the dust off a wig, placed it on the bald pumpkin head, and topped the manikin off with a dusty three-cornered hat.

"He needs a final touch," she said to the cat.

Dickon disappeared through the open back door. There was a loud *"Squawk!"* from the rooster in the yard outside. A moment later, the cat returned with a long tail feather in his jaws.

"The perfect touch!" exclaimed Mother Rigby. She stuck the feather in the dusty hat, then stood back to admire her creation. "Why," she said after a moment, "you're too fine a piece of work to stand in the field frightening crows and blackbirds."

Now she was a good-natured person, by and large, and loved to laugh. "I think we have the start of a wonderful joke here," she chuckled to Dickon. "I'll carry the illusion a little further, and turn my scarecrow into a man." She reached up and snatched her magic pipe out of thin air. Dickon mewed to let her know that breakfast, not a joke, was what interested him most, but she ignored him.

The witch blew a puff of sweet-smelling smoke into the scarecrow's pumpkin face. The blue swirls drifted through the vacant eyes and grinning mouth to fill the empty head.

Suddenly, there was the faintest twitch of the carved lips, the jerk of a wooden limb. The scarecrow took a wobbly step. Then another. Every time, he became more sure-footed.

"That's the spirit, my boy," urged Mother Rigby.

With each new step the puppet's wooden appearance turned more human, while his tattered clothing became as new as if it had just come from a tailor's shop.

"Now that you look like a man," said the old witch, sending a final puff of blue smoke swirling around her creation, "let me hear you speak!"

"Whatever you wish, Mother," responded the figure.

"Oh, you're the best puppet I've ever made!" cried the witch delightedly. "I love you more than any other I've conjured."

"And I love you with all my heart," said the figure, clasping his hand to his breast.

At this, Mother Rigby whooped with pleasure. "Now, my darling, I'm going to send you to call on Judge Gookin. The man doesn't like witches, and, though I've done him no mischief, he's given me nothing but trouble. It's time I gave him a little grief in return."

As she spoke, the old witch paced back and forth across the cottage floor. The transformed scarecrow, not having anything better to do, followed her, matching her step for step. Dickon watched the two of them curiously.

"The high-and-mighty Gookin has a beautiful daughter," said the witch, stopping so suddenly that her creation nearly stumbled into her. "You are handsome, and have wit and grace enough to win Polly Gookin's heart."

The figure, which now had beautiful deep blue eyes, gave a polite bow and said sincerely, "Never fear, Mother, I'll charm her if any gentleman can."

Mother Rigby realized that her creation was beginning to believe he was what he only seemed to be. "No matter," she muttered to herself, unable to look him in the eye. "It will just make the spell stronger."

She had her pipe in her left hand; with her right she called a bit of kindling from the fireplace. This she placed in the manikin's hand, where it instantly became a silver-headed cane.

"This will guide you to Judge Gookin's door, and the heart of my little joke," she chuckled. "Oh, if anyone should ask your name, say 'It is Feathertop,' for you have a handsome feather in your cap, and it seems a fitting name. Now, go!" she commanded her obedient and trusting servant.

So Feathertop left Mother Rigby's cottage, guided by the magic cane. As he strolled along, the townspeople admired his noble bearing, his rich clothes, his elegant cane, and his hat with the jaunty feather riding on it.

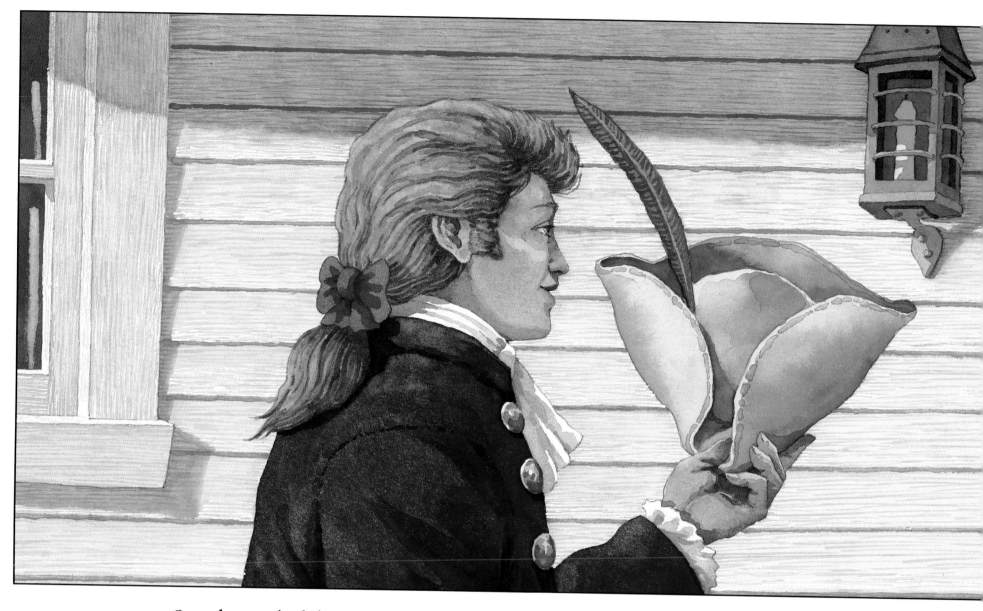

Soon he reached the mansion of Judge Gookin, and tapped politely on the front door.

Polly Gookin herself opened the door. She had seen the handsome Feathertop from her window, had managed a quick primping in the mirror on the landing, and had still reached the door before the maid. She was wearing a fine lace cap and held a dainty lace handkerchief, which she fluttered prettily.

"Mistress Gookin," said her visitor, bowing low and kissing her hand, "Feathertop is at your service."

She immediately invited Feathertop inside. But, for a moment, he could only stand and stare into her sea-green eyes and her fair, rosy face. He was enchanted, and followed her into the parlor like a man in a dream.

But the spell was broken when Judge Gookin clomped heavily down the hall and demanded, "What is the disturbance? I need quiet so I can finish reviewing my legal papers."

"This gentleman is Master Feathertop," Polly said quickly.

Feathertop bowed deeply. "I have come to call on your daughter."

The older man glanced approvingly at the newcomer—from his shining silver shoe buckles to the tip of his hat feather. "Well," the judge said, "please make yourself comfortable, and excuse me while I return to my paperwork."

When he left, Polly gestured her visitor toward the settee. She sat herself on a ladder-back chair near the sunny window. After a few awkward starts, followed by even more awkward silences, the two were soon deep in conversation.

But whenever Polly asked Feathertop about himself, Feathertop always turned her questions around, so that Polly ended up talking about herself.

Now the young woman very quickly found she was beginning to fall in love with the handsome Feathertop. At the same time, Feathertop was so charmed by her that he forgot his birth from straw and sticks and rags. He imagined himself a gallant suitor for Polly's hand, and not the pawn in Mother Rigby's careless joke.

Carried away with emotion, he fell to his knee and pleaded, "Give me just a nod, dear Polly, and I'll ask your father for your hand in marriage."

Polly blushed and fluttered her handkerchief for a moment, but she whispered, "Oh, yes, my Feathertop."

Then she took his hand and said, "Come with me. We're going to tell Father our good news."

But while they climbed the steps to the second floor like two happy children, Feathertop chanced to look in the full-length mirror on the landing. To his horror, he didn't see his human form reflected; instead, he saw Mother Rigby's patchwork of sticks and witchcraft.

Instantly, he remembered what he was and why he had come to Judge Gookin's house.

While Polly looked on in surprise from the head of the stairs, Feathertop threw up his arms in despair. Then he gave a fully human cry of pain and fled from the house, leaving Polly weeping tears of puzzlement and loss.

Feathertop ran back to Mother Rigby's cottage. There he found the witch sitting by her kitchen hearth, with Dickon curled up in her lap. But she jumped up when Feathertop burst into the room, tears streaming down his face.

"What has gone wrong?" demanded Mother Rigby. "Did Judge Gookin throw you out of his house? Why, I'll call up twenty devils to torment him, until he offers you his daughter on his bended knee!"

"No," said Feathertop miserably, "it wasn't that."

"Did the girl refuse you, then?" asked the witch, her eyes glowing like twin coals. "I'll punish her so—"

"NO!" cried Feathertop. "She was half-won, and—oh!—I think a kiss from her sweet lips might have made me truly human. But"—he sobbed, burying his face in his hands— "I've seen what a wretched, ragged, empty thing I am! I don't want to be alive any longer!"

"Poor Feathertop!" sighed Mother Rigby. "You have too much heart and feeling to be content as a puppet. Well, well, I'll make a scarecrow of you after all. It's probably for the best."

Mother Rigby gestured, then watched with regret as Feathertop sank into a pile of straw and tatters, with a shriveled pumpkin in the middle. Only the carved smile still had something human about it. Dickon batted playfully at the jaunty feather that rose from the ruin.

With a wave of the witch's hand, Feathertop's remains flew out the kitchen door and reassembled themselves in the field behind the cottage.

In the days that followed, Feathertop proved to make a poor scarecrow. His forlorn shape attracted the crows and blackbirds. They perched on his hat and shoulders, chattering among themselves, and sometimes took a bit of straw from his chest or a thread from his coat back to their nests. Mother Rigby muttered to Dickon often about discarding the scarecrow altogether, but something kept her from doing this.

Meanwhile, Polly Gookin could not forget the handsome stranger who had captured her heart, only to vanish so mysteriously. More and more, she sadly wandered the quiet lanes near Mother Rigby's cottage. As she often did, the young woman paused in front of Feathertop one evening. The lonely figure seemed to draw her to its side.

"Poor scarecrow," she sighed, stretching out her fingers to touch the tree branch that was his right hand. "You are so lucky! You've never fallen in love, only to have the one you love run away. Yet, even so, I sense a sadness in you that echoes my own. And I feel more at peace here than anywhere else, my dear, silent friend."

Mother Rigby, who had been watching through her open back door, hobbled toward the girl, with Dickon trotting at her heels.

"What's troubling you, child?" asked the old woman.

At first the girl was frightened, because her father had often warned her never to speak to the witch. But something kind in Mother Rigby's eyes reassured her. "I had a love," Polly sighed, "but he ran away. Still, I can't get him out of my heart. My father says the man was a wizard who bewitched me," she said in a whisper, afraid her words might offend the other woman.

"If there's magic afoot, it's the magic of love," said Mother Rigby, "and *you* are the source."

"I'm not a witch!" Polly said, startled.

"All people in love are witches and wizards," the old woman answered softly.

"If only that were true," said the young woman, "I'd kiss my scarecrow friend and turn him into my darling Feathertop this instant."

"Then do it, child," urged Mother Rigby.

The girl looked deep into the old woman's eyes, and Mother Rigby nodded encouragement. Suddenly, Polly grabbed the scarecrow's wooden hand and kissed it, crying, "Come back to me, dear Feathertop!"

At the same instant, Mother Rigby exhaled a puff of smoke from her magic pipe. The smoke grew as big as a cloud and soon covered everything.

Polly gasped in surprise. And when the smoke cleared, the scarecrow had vanished. But there was Feathertop, exactly as Polly remembered him, kneeling in front of her, gallantly kissing her hand.

"Dear Feathertop," said Polly, urging him to his feet, "I don't know where you've come from, but you must promise me you'll never go away again. I couldn't stand to lose you twice."

"Never," he answered gently. He stared deep into the sea-green mirrors of her eyes, but all he saw reflected there was a man as deep in love as a mortal man could be.

"Then come along with me," she said, taking his hand. And Feathertop joyfully followed her back toward town.

In the twilight, Mother Rigby watched the two departing figures. "Well, Dickon," she said, "each step walks him out of his old existence and into a new life. He'll forget me," she sighed, "but he'll no longer have to fear looking in a mirror."

She started back toward her cottage. "Tomorrow, Dickon," she called to the cat, who scampered ahead of her along the path, "we build a new scarecrow. But there'll be no dabbling in magic while I'm doing it—you have my word on that!"

Though cats can't laugh, Dickon managed a grin that served quite as well.

SAN   San Souci, Robert D.
           Feathertop

$16.00   39545000658640

DATE			
OCT 3 '94			